ITEM

D1434273

UXBRIDGE COLLEGE LEARNING CENTRE
Park Road, Uxbridge, Middlesex UB8 1NQ
Telephone: 01895 853326

Please return this item to the Learning Centre on
or before the last date stamped below:

DICKENS, C.   *Easy Reader*
A Christmas carol

1
Marley's Ghost

Marley was dead, to begin with. As dead as a doornail. There must be no doubt whatever about that. The register of his burial was signed by the clergyman, the clerk, the undertaker, and the chief mourner. Ebenezer Scrooge signed it, and Scrooge's name was good for anything he put it to.

Scrooge and Jacob Marley were partners for I don't know how many years. They were also friends, in their way. Scrooge never painted out Marley's name and there it stood, years afterwards, above the warehouse door: Scrooge and Marley. Sometimes people new to the firm called Scrooge Scrooge, and sometimes they called him Marley, but he answered to either. It was all the same to him.

Oh, but Scrooge was a tight-fisted, squeezing, wrenching, clutching, grasping old sinner! Hard and sharp as flint, he was, and as secretive and solitary as an oyster. The cold within him froze his old features, nipped his pointed nose, shrivelled his cheek, made his eyes red, his thin lips blue, and when he spoke it was with a harsh, grating voice.

Nobody ever stopped Scrooge in the street with a cheery, 'My dear Scrooge, how are you? When will you come to see me?' No beggars implored him for a coin, no children asked the time of him, no man or woman ever inquired the way to this place or that. But did Scrooge care? He did not, for this was the way he liked it.

Well let us begin. One Christmas Eve, old Scrooge sat busy in his counting-house. It was cold, bleak, biting weather, and he could hear the people outside wheezing by, beating their hands upon their chests and stamping their feet upon the pavement to warm them. The city clocks had only just gone three, but it was quite dark already, and candles flared in the windows of neighbouring offices. Fog came pouring in at every chink and keyhole, and was so dense outside that the houses opposite were mere phantoms.

The door of Scrooge's office was open, that he might keep an eye upon his clerk, Bob Cratchit. Scrooge had a very small fire, but Bob's was so much smaller that it looked like a single coal. Yet he could not

build it up, for his employer kept the coal-
box in his own room.

'A merry Christmas, uncle!' cried a
cheery voice. It was Scrooge's nephew,
Fred, who had come in so quickly that this
was the first Scrooge knew of his approach.

'Bah!' said Scrooge. 'Humbug!'

Fred had become so heated with rapid
walking in the cold fog that he was all
aglow. His eyes sparkled and there was
smoke upon his every breath.

'Christmas a humbug, uncle?' he cried. 'You don't mean that, I'm sure!'

'I do,' said Scrooge. 'Merry Christmas! What reason have you to be merry? You're poor enough.'

'What reason have you to be so gloomy?' Fred replied gaily. 'You're rich enough.'

'Bah!' said Scrooge again, and, once more: 'Humbug! Merry Christmas indeed,' he continued. 'If I had my way every idiot who goes about with "Merry Christmas" on his lips would be boiled with his own pudding, and buried with a stake of holly through his heart!'

'Uncle Scrooge,' said Fred. 'Come! Dine with us tomorrow. Be a little merry for once.'

'Merry!' said Scrooge and stamped his foot. 'Good afternoon!'

His nephew sighed. 'I'm sorry you're so determined, but I'll keep my Christmas humour to the last. Merry Christmas, uncle!'

'Good afternoon, I say!'

Fred left the room without an angry word, but stopped at the outer door to bestow the season's greetings on the clerk, who, cold as he was, returned them warmly.

'There's another fellow,' muttered

Scrooge: 'Bob Cratchit, with fifteen shillings a week, and a wife and family, talking about a merry Christmas. Two fools together.'

As the clerk let the nephew out, two others stepped in. These two gentlemen stood with their hats off in Scrooge's office, smiling pleasantly and bowing to him.

'Scrooge and Marley's, I believe,' said one. 'Have we the pleasure of addressing Mr Scrooge or Mr Marley?'

'Mr Marley is dead,' Scrooge snapped. 'He died seven years ago this very night.'

'Well then, Mr Scrooge. We are gathering donations for the poor and destitute, who suffer greatly at this time of year. I'm sure you know that thousands are in want of ordinary comforts.'

'Are there no prisons?' asked Scrooge.

'Why yes,' the gentleman answered, surprised. 'Plenty of prisons.'

'And are there no workhouses?' asked Scrooge.

'There are, sir.' It was the second visitor who replied to this. 'I wish I could say that there were not.'

'Oh! I was afraid that they had been closed down while my back was turned.'

'Would you care to make a contribution?'

one of the gentlemen inquired, a little
nervously.

'No, sir, I would not,' Scrooge replied.
'I don't make merry myself at Christmas,
and I can't afford to make idle people
merry. Good afternoon to you both!'

Seeing that it would be useless to argue,
the gentlemen withdrew. Scrooge picked
up his pen and continued with his work.

While he worked on, the fog and
darkness thickened and the church tower
beyond his window became invisible. Foggier
yet, it became, and colder! Piercing,
searching, biting cold. At length the hour
of shutting up the counting-house arrived.
With some reluctance, Scrooge admitted
this to his clerk, who instantly snuffed his

candle out and put on his hat and coat.

'You'll want all day off tomorrow, I suppose?' said Scrooge.

'If it's convenient, sir,' replied Bob.

'It is not convenient, and it's not fair. How fair would you think it if I were to stop you a day's money for it, eh?'

'It is only one day a year, sir.'

'A poor excuse for picking a man's pocket every twenty-fifth of December!' Scrooge buttoned his coat to the chin. 'Well, make sure to be here all the earlier next morning.'

From the office, Scrooge walked to his usual melancholy tavern for a melancholy dinner. Then, after reading the newspapers, he took himself off home.

He lived in a gloomy old house which had once belonged to his partner, Jacob Marley. The fog hung so thickly about the gateway, and the yard was so dark, that Scrooge was obliged to grope with his hands. An odd shiver might have passed down even his icy old spine this night, as well it might with all that was to come.

Now it is a fact that there was nothing at all peculiar about the knocker on the door of Scrooge's house, except that it was very large. Scrooge had seen this knocker,

night and morning, during his whole
residence there. It should also be borne in
mind that he had given not a moment's
thought to Jacob Marley since the last
mention of his name that afternoon. And
yet, as Scrooge inserted his key in the lock,
he saw not a knocker, but ... a face.

Marley's face.

The face in the knocker was not in
thick shadow, as were the other objects in
the yard, but had a dismal light about it.
Its colour was a bluish grey and, though it
did not appear angry or ferocious, it had a
ghostly air, with ghostly spectacles raised
upon a ghostly forehead.

Scrooge stared at the pale face of his
long dead partner. And as he stared, it
became a knocker again.

To say that he was not startled by all this would be untrue, but Scrooge was not a man to be halted by things he did not understand. He turned the key, walked in, and lit a candle. He paused a moment before shutting the door, but then called himself an old fool, closed it with a bang, and fastened it. He walked across the hall and up the broad dark staircase. Scrooge did not mind the dark. Darkness was cheap.

He closed his bedroom door and locked himself in; double-locked it, which was not his usual custom. He then put on his dressing gown and his slippers and his nightcap, and sat down before the fire to warm himself. It was a very low fire for such a bitter night, and he was forced to sit close to it to gain any benefit. But as he sat, hands stretched out before him, a face rose up where flames should be and stared at him.

Scrooge fell back in his chair. But then, collecting himself, he cried 'Humbug!' and got up and walked across the room.

After several turns about the room he sat down again. As he threw his head back in the chair, his glance fell upon an ancient bell that hung on the wall. Scrooge never used this bell; it had simply always been there.

But as he looked at it, the bell, to his great astonishment, began to swing. It swung so softly at first that it scarcely made a sound; but soon it was ringing loudly, as was every other bell in the house.

This great ringing from all quarters might have lasted but a minute, yet it seemed an hour. And then the bells stopped, all at once, all together. The silence that followed was brief, however, for then came a clanking noise from down below, as if someone were dragging a heavy chain over a stone floor.

But this was not the worst of it, for a door below flew open with a booming sound, and then he heard the noise, the terrible clanking noise, coming up the stairs; then coming straight towards his door.

'It's humbug still!' said Scrooge. 'I won't believe it.'

His colour changed though, when, without a pause, a figure stepped through the locked and bolted door and stood before his eyes. A large handkerchief was bound about its head and chin, as if to hold the jaw in place. Its body was transparent, so that Scrooge could see the two buttons on its coat behind. Around its middle the chain was clasped: long, and wound about him like a tail, and made of cash-boxes, keys, padlocks, ledgers, and heavy steel purses.

As you may imagine, this spectre disturbed Scrooge to the very marrow of his bones. Yet he determined not to show it.

'What do you want with me?' he inquired coldly.

'Do you recognize me, Ebenezer?' the Ghost replied in mournful tones. 'I was in life your partner, Jacob Marley.'

'I recognize who you appear to be,' said Scrooge. 'Can you sit down? If so, pray do so.'

The Spectre seated itself at the opposite end of the fireplace. 'You don't believe in me,' it observed.

'I don't,' said Scrooge.

'Why do you doubt your senses?'

'Because any little thing affects them. Any slight disorder of the stomach. You may be an undigested bit of beef, a blot of mustard, a crumb of cheese, a fragment of underdone potato. There's more of gravy than grave about you, whatever you are!'

At this, the Spirit raised a frightful cry, and shook its chain with such a dismal and appalling noise, that Scrooge gripped his chair to save himself from falling in a faint. Ah, but how much greater was his horror when the Phantom removed the bandage from its head and its lower jaw dropped down upon its breast!

Scrooge fell upon his knees and clasped his hands before his face. 'Mercy! Dreadful apparition, why do you trouble me?'

'So you do believe in me,' the Phantom replied.

'I do,' said Scrooge. 'I must. Jacob! Tell me why you are here. Comfort me!'

'I bring no comfort,' returned the mournful Ghost. 'Like you, I led a miserable penny-pinching life, and in death I rove from here to there in the chains I made for myself on earth. I come tonight to warn you, Ebenezer; warn you that, if you truly wish it, you may yet escape my fate.'

'I thank you,' said Scrooge carefully. 'You were always a good friend to me.'

'You will be haunted,' said the Ghost, 'by three Spirits.'

'Is that the chance you mentioned, Jacob? To be haunted, and thrice over?'

'Without their visits you will tread the path I tread, rattle your chains alongside mine.'

'Couldn't I take 'em all at once,' asked Scrooge, 'and have it over with?'

'Expect the first Spirit tomorrow when the bell tolls one,' said Marley's Ghost. 'Expect the second on the next night at the same hour. The third will come the following night when twelve has struck. You will see me no more, Ebenezer, but remember, for your own sake, all that has passed between us!'

With this the Spectre bound up its head as before and rose from its chair. Then, winding the great chain over its arm, it walked away, backward, towards the window.

At its every step, the window raised itself a little, so that it was wide open by the time the Phantom reached it. It beckoned to Scrooge to approach.

Scrooge became aware of confused sounds of misery and regret outside, of sorrowful, self-pitying wailings. The Spectre, after listening for a moment, joined in the mournful dirge and floated out upon the bleak, dark night.

Scrooge looked out. The air was filled with phantoms, wandering here and there in restless haste, moaning as they went. Every one wore chains like Marley's Ghost. Whether these creatures dissolved into mist, Scrooge could not tell, but their voices and bodies faded together, and the night became as it had been when he walked home.

Scrooge closed the window. He tried to say 'Humbug!' but stopped at the first syllable. Then a great weariness overtook him and he went straight to bed without undressing, and fell instantly asleep.

What do we learn about Scrooge's character from this chapter?

2
The First
of the Three Spirits

When Scrooge awoke it was so dark that,
from his bed, he could hardly tell the
window from the walls of his room. He was
endeavouring to do so with his ferret eyes
when the chimes of a neighbouring church
clock began to strike. He counted the
strikes, and to his great astonishment the
heavy bell went all the way to twelve before
stopping. Twelve! But how? It was past two
when he went to bed.

'Why, it isn't possible,' said Scrooge,
'that I can have slept through a whole day
and far into another night!'

He scrambled out of bed and groped
his way to the window. He was obliged to
rub the frost off with the sleeve of his
dressing gown before he could see
anything, and even then all he could make
out was that the fog was still very thick.

Scrooge returned to his bed, and
thought, and thought, and thought again,
and could make nothing of it. Marley's

Ghost bothered him greatly. Every time he decided that the Phantom had come to him in a dream, his mind turned again, and he was no longer sure.

He lay in this confused state until the clock chimed three-quarters more, when all of a sudden he remembered that the Ghost had warned him to expect a visit at one o'clock. Scrooge waited expectantly for the chime, and at length it came, a single deep, dull, melancholy note. At once, light flared up in the room, and Scrooge found himself face to face with an unearthly visitor.

It was a strange figure – like a child, yet also like an old man shrunk to a child's proportions. Its hair, which hung down its back, was white as if with age, yet the face had not a wrinkle in it. The Spirit wore a tunic of the purest white, and round its waist a lustrous belt which shone with great beauty. The tunic was trimmed with summer flowers, yet in its hand the child-man held a branch of fresh green winter holly.

But the strangest thing about the apparition was the bright clear jet of light that sprang from its head and made all this visible. Under its arm it held a great cap, which it doubtless used to put out the light when it wished to be dull.

'Are you the Spirit whose coming was foretold to me?' asked Scrooge.

'I am.'

'Who and what are you?'

'I am the Ghost of Christmas Past.'

'How long past?'

'Your past.' The Spirit put out its hand and grasped his arm. 'Rise! Walk with me!'

The grasp, though gentle, was not to be resisted. Scrooge rose, but finding that the Spirit made for the window, he clasped its robe to hold it back.

'Spirit, I am but mortal, and liable to fall.'

The Spirit laid a hand on Scrooge's heart. 'A touch of my hand there and you shall not fall, here or anywhere.'

As these words were spoken they passed through the wall, and on the other side Scrooge found himself not falling through the air, as he might have expected, but on an open country road, with fields on either side. The city had vanished, and the foggy dark with it, for it was a clear, cold winter day, with snow upon the ground.

'Good heavens!' said Scrooge as he looked about him. 'I know this place. I was a boy here!'

The Spirit gazed upon him mildly. 'Do you remember the way?'

'Remember it! I could walk it blindfold.'

'Strange then to have given it so little thought for so many years,' observed the Ghost.

They walked along the road, Scrooge recognizing every gate and post and tree, until a little market town appeared in the distance, with its bridge, its church, and winding river. Some ponies were trotting towards them with boys on their backs, who called to other boys in carts driven by farmers. These lads were all in high spirits, shouting to each other until the fields were so merry that even the crisp December air seemed to laugh.

'Can they see us?' asked Scrooge. 'Can they hear us?'

'These are but shadows of things that have been,' replied the Ghost. 'They are not aware of us.'

Scrooge watched the travellers pass by. He knew these boys, every one; could name them all. His cold eye glistened and his wintry heart leapt as they went past. Indeed, he was filled with gladness when he heard them wish each other Merry Christmas, as they parted at crossroads and byways. Strange, very strange, for what was Christmas to Ebenezer Scrooge? What good had it ever done him?

'The school is not quite deserted,' said the Ghost. 'A solitary child, neglected by his friends, is there still.'

'The school?' said Scrooge. 'What child?'

'Come,' said the Spirit.

They left the high road by a lane that Scrooge remembered well, and soon approached a mansion of dull red brick with a school bell upon the roof. It was a large house, but one of broken fortunes.

The walls were damp and mossy, and a number of the windows were broken. Entering the dreary hall, Scrooge and the Ghost of Christmas Past glanced through open doors into many a cold and poorly furnished room.

They came to a door at the back of the house. The door opened before them and revealed a long, high, bare room, made all the more melancholy by rows of plain benches and desks. A boy sat reading by a feeble fire.

'Why,' cried Scrooge, 'it is myself!'

He sat down nearby and a tear came into his eye to see his poor forgotten self as he used to be, left here all alone for the Christmas holiday.

'Poor boy,' he whispered. 'Poor lonely, unwanted boy.'

The Ghost smiled thoughtfully and waved its hand. 'Let us see another Christmas!'

Scrooge's former self grew larger at these words, and the room became a little darker and more dirty. The wood panels shrank, more windows cracked, fragments of plaster fell from the ceiling. Young Ebenezer, though older, was alone again. He was not reading now, but walking up and down despairingly. Old Scrooge, with a mournful shaking of the head, glanced anxiously towards the door.

It opened, and a small girl, much younger than the boy, came darting in. Putting her arms about his neck and kissing him, she addressed him as her 'dear, dear brother.'

'Ebenezer, I've come to bring you home!' she said, clapping her hands and laughing. 'To bring you home, home, *home*!'

'Home, little Fan?' returned the boy, puzzled.

'Yes!' said the child, brimful of glee. 'Home for good and all. Home for ever and ever. Father is so much kinder than he used to be, and home's like heaven!

He spoke so gently to me one night when I was going to bed that I was not afraid to ask him once more if you might come home. And he said that you could, and sent me in a coach to bring you. And you are never to come back here, and we are to be together all the Christmas long, and have the merriest time in all the world!'

She clapped her hands again and again and laughed, and stood on tiptoe to embrace him. Then she began to drag him eagerly towards the door; and he accompanied her with pleasure.

In the hall, the schoolmaster called for Master Scrooge's trunk to be brought down. While this was being done, he led the boy and his sister to the parlour, where he gave them a tot of light wine and a piece of cake. Once the trunk was tied to the top of the coach, the children bade the schoolmaster goodbye and drove gaily away. Scrooge and the Spirit heard the girl's delighted laughter as they went.

'Always a delicate creature,' said the Ghost. 'But she had a large heart.'

'So she had,' Scrooge murmured tenderly. 'So she had.'

'She died a woman,' said the Ghost,

'and had, I think, one child.'

'Yes,' Scrooge answered with some unease. 'Fred, my nephew.'

Scrooge and the Spirit also left the school behind, but for the city. Here, too, it was Christmas, but it was evening, and the streets and shops were well lit up. The Ghost stopped at a certain warehouse door and asked Scrooge if he knew it.

'Know it!' said Scrooge. 'I was apprenticed here!'

They went in. Inside they found an old gentleman sitting behind a desk so high that, if he had been two inches taller, he would have knocked his head against the ceiling.

'Why, it's old Fezziwig!' cried Scrooge in great excitement. 'Bless his heart, Fezziwig alive again!'

Mr Fezziwig looked at the clock, which pointed to the hour of seven, and laid down his pen. He rubbed his hands, adjusted his waistcoat, and called out in a comfortable, rich, fat, jovial voice:

'Yo ho, there! Ebenezer! Dick!'

Scrooge's former self, now grown into a young man, came briskly in, accompanied by his fellow apprentice.

'Dick Wilkins!' Scrooge exclaimed. 'Bless me if it isn't.' He glanced at the Spirit. 'Very much attached to me, was young Dick.'

'Christmas Eve, my boys!' said Mr Fezziwig, skipping down from his high desk. 'No more work tonight! Clear away, lads! Let's have lots of room here!'

In a minute the office furniture was packed away, the floor was swept, the lamps trimmed, and fuel heaped upon the fire. Soon the warehouse was as snug and warm and bright a room as you could wish to see upon a winter's night.

Then in came a fiddler and went up to the lofty desk, and tuned up his instrument with a noise like fifty stomach-aches. In came Mrs Fezziwig, all smiles. In came the three Miss Fezziwigs, beaming and lovable. In came their six young followers whose hearts they broke. In came all the young men and women employed in the business. In came the housemaid with her cousin the baker. In came the cook with her brother's friend the milkman. In came the boy from over the way, trying to hide himself behind the girl from next door but one.

In they all came, one after another, some shyly, some boldly, some gracefully. In they came and away they went, twenty of them at once, in a merry old dance down the middle of the room; down and up and down again, and round and round and round again, until it was time for the feasting to begin. And then – why, more dancing!

During all this, Scrooge, standing with the Spirit, acted like a man who'd lost his wits. His heart and soul were in the scene as he remembered everything, enjoyed everything, became at least as agitated as his younger self.

When the clock struck eleven, Mr and Mrs Fezziwig took their places at either side of the door, and, shaking hands with everyone as he or she went out, wished him or her a Merry Christmas. When all the cheerful voices had died away and the lights been snuffed out, the two apprentices went happily to their beds under the counter in the back of the shop. The Spirit signed to Scrooge to listen to their whispered praise of their master, Mr Fezziwig.

'A small matter,' said the Ghost, 'to make these silly folk so grateful.'

'Small!' echoed Scrooge.

'Certainly. He spent but a few pounds. Is that so much that he deserves such praise?'

'It isn't that,' said Scrooge. 'Old Fezziwig had the power to render us happy or unhappy, make our days light or heavy, a pleasure or a toil. The happiness he gave was as great as if it had cost him a fortune.'

He felt the Spirit's glance, and stopped.

'What is the matter?' asked the Ghost.

'I should like to be able to say a word or two to my clerk just now, that's all.'

His younger self turned down the lamps as he uttered this wish, and Scrooge and the Ghost stood side by side in the open air.

'My time grows short,' observed the Spirit. 'Quick!'

This was not addressed to Scrooge, or to anyone he could see, but it produced an immediate effect. For again Scrooge saw himself. He was older again, a man now, in the prime of life. His face had not the harsh and rigid lines of later years, but it had begun to wear signs of care and greed.

He was not alone, but sat by the side of a fair young girl, in whose eyes there were tears.

'Belle!' said Scrooge softly. 'My Belle.'

'I matter little to you now, Ebenezer,' she said to his younger self beside her. 'Another idol has replaced me – a golden idol.'

'No,' the young man retorted. 'I have merely become wiser. There is nothing wrong with the pursuit of wealth.'

'It has changed you,' the girl said. 'Our agreement was made when we were both poor and content to be so. You were a different man then.'

'I was a boy,' he said impatiently.

'You are certainly not what you were, but I am the same as ever I was. We who were as one are now two, and unhappy together. It saddens me, but I must release you.'

'Release me? Have I ever sought release?'

'In words, no, but in your changed nature, oh certainly. I'm sure that today, with your great liking for the counting-house, you would not choose a girl such as I, who has neither money nor property. There would be no gain in such a marriage.'

'Oh, I don't know about that,' the young man said, but he spoke hesitantly.

'I think that you do,' the girl replied, looking him full in the face. 'And because of it I say again, you are released from your vow. You are free, Ebenezer, to gather the wealth that you desire. And may you be happy in the life you have chosen!'

With that she left him; and they parted.

'Spirit!' cried Scrooge. 'Show me no more! Why do you delight in torturing me? Take me home.'

'One shadow more!' said the Ghost.

And they were instantly in another place: a room, not large or particularly handsome, but very comfortable. Near to the winter fire sat a beautiful girl, so like the last that Scrooge believed it was the same, until he saw *her*, not quite middle-aged, sitting opposite her daughter. The noise in the room was tumultuous, for there were more children than might easily be counted and every child behaved like forty, each making forty's noise. It surprised Scrooge that the mother and daughter did not scold or hush the unruly herd. Quite the contrary. They laughed heartily at all the racket.

A knock came at the door, and such a rush was there to answer it. A man entered, laden with Christmas presents for all. Oh, the shouts of wonder and delight with which each packet was received!

Scrooge gazed on attentively as the master of the house sat down with his daughter and her mother at the fireside.

'I saw an old friend of yours this afternoon, Belle,' he said.

'Oh, who?'

'Why, Mr Scrooge. I passed his office window, and as there was a candle inside I could scarcely help seeing him. His partner lies on the point of death, I hear, and there he sat, still working away. He's quite alone in the world now, I believe.'

Scrooge turned upon the Ghost. Its light was very bright. It seemed to Scrooge that the light burned higher and brighter with each new misery he was shown.

'Spirit!' he wailed. 'Remove me from this place, I cannot bear it.'

'These are shadows of things that have been,' said the Ghost. 'Do not blame me that they are what they are.'

Seeing that the Ghost was undisturbed by his pleas, Scrooge seized the extinguisher-cap and pressed it down upon its head. The Ghost dropped beneath it until the cap covered its whole form.

Then Scrooge, overcome by a sudden drowsiness, noticed that he was once again in his own bedroom. He gave the cap a parting squeeze and had barely time to reel to his bed, before he sank into a heavy sleep.

How did Scrooge celebrate Christmas when he was younger?

Why was Scrooge upset by the 'shadows' of his past?

3

The Second
of the Three Spirits

Waking in the middle of a particularly
sharp snore, and sitting up in bed to get
his thoughts together, Scrooge had no
need to be told that the church bell was
once again about to make the stroke of
one. He felt that he'd been brought to
consciousness in the nick of time, for the
special purpose of meeting the second
messenger promised by Jacob Marley.

The prospect turned him
uncomfortably cold, and he lay back
wondering what fearsome shape this new
apparition might take. He prepared himself
for anything, so that soon he was ready for
such a range of strange appearances that
nothing between a baby and a rhinoceros
would have astonished him very much.

The one thing Scrooge failed to
prepare himself for was nothing – nothing
but the blaze of light that streamed upon
his bed when the clock struck one. At this,
he was taken with a violent fit of trembling.

Being only light, it alarmed him more than a dozen ghosts, as he was powerless to make out what it might do.

At last, however, he began to think that the secret of this ghostly light might be in the adjoining room, from which it seemed to shine. He got up softly and shuffled in his slippers to the door. As he approached, a strange voice called him by name and bade him enter. He peeked in.

It was his own room. There was no doubt about that. But it had undergone a startling transformation. The walls and ceiling were so hung with living greenery that it looked like a perfect grove, from every part of which bright berries glistened. The crisp leaves of holly, mistletoe and ivy reflected back the light as if so many mirrors had been scattered there, and such a mighty blaze roared up the chimney as that dull hearth had never known in Scrooge's time, or Marley's before him.

Heaped up on the floor, forming a kind of throne, were turkeys, geese, great joints of meat, long wreaths of sausages, mince pies, plum puddings, hot chestnuts, cherry-cheeked apples, juicy oranges, luscious pears, and seething bowls of

punch that steamed deliciously.

Upon this throne there sat a jolly giant, glorious to see, who held aloft a glowing torch that shed its light on Scrooge as he came peeping round the door.

'Come in!' exclaimed the Ghost. 'Come in and know me better, man!'

Scrooge entered timidly and hung his head before the jolly Spirit. Of all things he had been ready for, none had shaped themselves like this, and though the Spirit's eyes were clear and kind he did not care to meet them.

'I am the Ghost of Christmas Present,' said the Spirit. 'Look upon me!'

Scrooge did so, very humbly. The Spirit was clothed in a simple green robe bordered with white fur. This garment hung so loosely that its enormous chest was bare. Its feet, visible beneath the ample folds, were also bare. On its head the Spirit wore a holly wreath set here and there with shining icicles. Its hair was long and free, as free as its genial face, its sparkling eye, its open hand, its cheery voice, its joyful air.

'You have never seen the like of me before, I think!' said the Spirit.

'Never,' said Scrooge. 'O Spirit, take me where you will. Last night I was compelled to go forth, and I learned a powerful lesson. Tonight, if you have aught to teach me, let me profit by it.'

'Touch my robe!'

Scrooge did as he was told, and held it fast.

Holly, mistletoe, red berries, ivy, turkeys, geese, meat, sausages, pies, puddings, chestnuts, fruit and punch, all vanished instantly. So did the room, the fire, the warm glow, even the hour of night, for they stood in the city streets on

Christmas morning.

The sky was gloomy and the streets were choked up with a dingy mist. Snow lay all about, on roof and wall and chimney pot, but dirty on the ground. There was nothing very cheerful in the climate or the town, and yet was there an air of cheerfulness that the brightest summer sun could not have improved upon.

People shovelling snow from roof and pavement were jovial and full of glee, calling out to one another and now and then exchanging a snowball, laughing heartily if it went right, and no less heartily if it went wrong. The poulterers' shops were still half open, and the fruiterers' were radiant. There were great round baskets of chestnuts, shaped like the waistcoats of jolly old gentlemen; there were pears and apples clustered high in ripe pyramids; there were bunches of grapes made to dangle from hooks that people's mouths might water as they passed; and oh, such a multitude of other delights poking out from the gloom!

And soon there emerged, from lanes and side streets and doorways, scores of people carrying their covered dinners to the bakers' shops for cooking. The sight of these poor souls appeared to interest the Spirit very much, for he took the covers off as they passed and sprinkled incense on the dinners from his torch.

'Is there a particular flavour in what you sprinkle from your torch?' asked Scrooge.

'There is,' answered the Ghost. 'My own.'

They went on, invisibly, into the suburbs of the town. And where did they go, but straight to the house of Scrooge's clerk, Bob Cratchit! There, the Spirit smiled and blessed the humble little house with a sprinkle of his torch.

Then in came Mrs Cratchit, dressed poorly but in ribbons to make a show of the season, while Master Peter Cratchit plunged a fork into a saucepan of potatoes. And now two smaller Cratchits, boy and girl, came tearing in, screaming that outside the baker's they had smelt the goose and known it for their own, and they danced about the table basking in luxurious thoughts of sage and onion.

'Wherever has your father got to?' said Mrs Cratchit. 'And Tiny Tim? And Martha weren't as late as this last Christmas Day.'

'Here's Martha, mother!' said a girl,

appearing as she spoke.

'Here's Martha, mother!' cried the two young Cratchits. 'Hurrah! And you should see our goose, Martha!'

'My dear, how late you are!' said Mrs Cratchit, kissing Martha a dozen times and taking off her shawl and bonnet for her.

'We'd a deal of work to finish up last night,' replied the girl, 'and had to clear away this morning.'

'Well, never mind so long as you've come. Sit down before the fire, now, and have a warm ...'

'No, no, here's father!' cried the two young Cratchits. 'Hide, Martha, hide!'

So Martha hid herself, and in came Bob Cratchit, his threadbare clothes all darned up, and his son, Tiny Tim, upon his shoulder. Alas for Tiny Tim, he bore a crutch, and had his limbs supported by an iron frame.

'Why, where's our Martha?' cried Bob, looking round.

'Not coming,' said Mrs Cratchit.

'Not coming?' Bob's face fell, for he had raced home from church in right high spirits with Tiny Tim upon his shoulder. 'Not coming on Christmas Day?'

Martha did not like to see her father
disappointed by a joke, so she came out
from behind the closet door and ran into
his arms, while the two young Cratchits
hustled Tiny Tim off to the wash-house
that he might hear the pudding singing on
the stove.

'And how did Tim behave?' asked Mrs
Cratchit when Bob had hugged his
daughter to his heart's content.

'As good as gold,' said Bob. 'He's a
lively little soul and no mistake, and
growing strong and hearty.'

His voice trembled as he said this, for
he spoke only half the truth. Before

another word was said, back came Tim, his active little crutch clattering on the floor, escorted by his brother and sister to his stool beside the fire.

Then, while Bob mixed up some hot mixture in a jug and put it on the hob to simmer, Master Peter and the two young Cratchits went to fetch the goose, with which they soon returned in a procession.

Such a bustle followed that you might have thought a goose the rarest of birds. Mrs Cratchit made the gravy, Master Peter mashed the potatoes with great vigour, Miss Belinda sweetened the apple sauce, Martha dusted the hot plates, and Bob sat Tiny Tim beside him at the table. The two young Cratchits set chairs for everyone and crammed spoons into their mouths lest they should shriek for goose before their helping came.

At last the dishes were set, and grace was said. It was followed by a breathless pause, as Mrs Cratchit, taking her time, prepared to plunge the carving knife in the goose's breast. And when she did, a murmur of delight arose, and even Tiny Tim beat on the table with the handle of his knife, and feebly cried 'Hurrah!'

Scrooge and the Ghost watched the carving of the goose without a word. They listened to the jolly family heap praise upon the mother for her work: 'The best goose that ever was cooked, my dear,' said Bob. They observed the eating of the feast, the clearing away of the plates, the bringing in of the pudding. Through all this, Scrooge's face was lit up like that of a welcome guest in this happy house.

At last the dinner was done, the cloth was cleared, the fire made up. Apples and oranges were put upon the table and a shovel full of chestnuts on the fire. Then all the Cratchit family drew round the hearth. The mixture in the jug was tasted and pronounced perfect, and Bob served it out while the chestnuts sputtered and cracked noisily. Then he raised his glass and proposed a toast.

'A Merry Christmas to us all, my dears! God bless us!'

Which all the family echoed.

'God bless us every one!' said Tiny Tim, the last of all.

He sat very close to his father on his little stool. Bob held his withered little hand, as if he wished to keep him by his side and dreaded that he might be taken from him.

'Spirit,' said Scrooge, with an interest he had never felt before, 'tell me if Tiny Tim will live.'

'I see a vacant seat in the chimney corner there,' replied the Ghost, 'and a crutch without an owner. If these shadows remain unaltered by the Future, the child will die.'

'No, no,' wailed Scrooge. 'Oh no, kind Spirit! Say he will be spared!'

'If these shadows remain unaltered by the Future,' the Spirit repeated, 'none will find him here.'

Scrooge trembled, overcome with grief, and cast his eyes upon the ground. But he raised them speedily on hearing his own name.

'Mr Scrooge!' said Bob Cratchit, raising his glass again. 'I give you Mr Scrooge, the founder of this wondrous feast!'

'The founder of this feast indeed!' cried his wife, reddening. 'I wish I had him here. I'd give him a piece of my mind to feast upon!'

'My dear,' said Bob, 'the children! Christmas Day.'

'It should be Christmas Day, I'm sure,' said she, 'on which one drinks the health of such an odious, stingy, hard, unfeeling man as Mr Scrooge. You know he is, Robert. Nobody knows it better than you!'

'My dear,' said Bob mildly.

'I'll drink his health for your sake and the Day's, not his,' said Mrs Cratchit, raising her glass. 'Long life to him! A Merry Christmas and a Happy New Year! He'll be very merry and happy, I have no doubt!'

The children drank the toast after her, but their hearts weren't in it. Scrooge was the ogre of the family. The mention of his name cast a dark shadow on the party. Scrooge observed all with a sorrowful eye. When the scene faded, he had this eye upon the family, and especially on Tiny Tim, until the last.

By this time it was getting dark, and snowing pretty heavily; and as Scrooge and the Spirit went along the streets, the brightness of the roaring fires in kitchens, parlours, and all sorts of rooms was wonderful. Here, the flickering of the blaze showed preparations for a cosy dinner, with deep red curtains ready to be drawn, to shut out cold and darkness. There, the

children of the house ran out into the snow
to greet their married sisters, brothers,
cousins, uncles, aunts. Even the lamplighter,
who ran round dotting the dusky street with
specks of light, laughed out loud as Scrooge
and the Spirit passed, though he knew not
that he had any company but Christmas.

And now, without a word of warning
from the Ghost, they stood upon a bleak,
deserted moor, where monstrous masses of
stone were cast about, as though it were the
burial place of giants. Water spread itself
wherever it wished, or would have done so
but for the frost that held it prisoner.
Nothing grew here but moss and gorse and
coarse grass. Down in the west, the setting
sun glared at this desolation for an instant
like a sullen eye; then, frowning lower,
lower, and lower yet, was lost in the gloom
of darkest night.

'What place is this?' asked Scrooge.

'A place where miners live,' returned
the Spirit. 'Come!'

A light shone from the window of a hut,
and they advanced towards it. Passing
through the wall of mud and stone, they
found a cheerful company assembled round
a glowing fire. An old, old man was singing

a Christmas song. It had been a very old song when he was a boy, and from time to time the others joined in the chorus.

The Spirit did not tarry here, but bade Scrooge hold his robe, and, passing on above the moor, sped out across the sea. To Scrooge's horror, looking back, he saw the last of the land behind them. And his ears were deafened by the thundering of water as it rolled and roared and raged.

They came upon a solitary lighthouse, built upon a dismal reef of sunken rocks. Great heaps of seaweed clung to its base, and storm-birds, born upon the wind, rose and fell about it like the waves they skimmed.

Even here, the two men who watched the light had made a fire that shed a ray of brightness on the awful sea. Joining hands over the rough table at which they sat, they wished each other Merry Christmas; and the elder of the two, his face all scarred with hard weather, struck up a sturdy song that was like a gale itself.

Again the Ghost sped on, above the black and heaving sea, on and on, until, far from any shore, they came down upon a ship. They stood beside the helmsman at the wheel, and the lookout in the bow, and the officers on watch, and every man among them hummed a Christmas tune, or had a Christmas thought, or spoke softly to his companion of some bygone Christmas Day.

It was a great surprise to Scrooge, while listening to the moaning of the wind and the crashing of the waves, to hear a sudden hearty laugh. It was a much greater surprise to him to recognize it as his own nephew's, and to find himself in a bright, dry, gleaming room, with the Spirit smiling at his side.

'Ha, ha!' laughed Fred. 'Ha, ha, ha!'

What a blessed laugh had Scrooge's nephew! What a noble, rollicking laugh! A laugh that any near must surely share. And share it they did, his wife and their assembled friends, holding their sides, rolling their heads, all roaring lustily.

'Ha, ha! Ha, ha, ha, ha!'

'He said Christmas was a humbug, as I

live and breathe!' cried the nephew. 'He believed it too!'

'Shame on him!' said his wife indignantly.

She was pretty, exceedingly pretty, with a dimpled, surprised-looking face, a ripe little mouth, with dimples all about her chin when she laughed, and the sunniest pair of eyes you ever saw.

'He's a comical old fellow,' said Fred, 'and not so pleasant as he might be. But he is my uncle and I'll say nothing against him.'

'I have no patience with him,' observed Scrooge's niece.

'I'm sorry for him,' said the nephew. 'I couldn't be angry with him if I tried. Who suffers by his ill temper? Himself, always. He takes it into his head to dislike us and won't come and dine with us. Well, it's he who loses a good dinner and some pleasant company, not us!'

And then they had some music. Much tuneful singing was there, and Scrooge's niece played well upon the harp. When this simple music sounded, all the things the Ghost had shown him came back into his mind. Scrooge softened more and more, and thought that if he had listened to such music years ago, and often since, he might have been a kinder and happier man.

The scene faded then, and Scrooge and the Ghost of Christmas Present were again upon their travels.

Much they saw, and far they went, and many homes they visited, but always with a happy end. The Spirit stood beside sick-beds, and the sick were cheerful; by struggling men, and they were patient and hopeful; by poverty, and it was rich. In hospital, in gaol, in the workhouse, in misery's every refuge, the Ghost left its blessing and hinted, for Scrooge's benefit, at the meaning of kindness and generosity.

It was a long night, a very long night, and as it passed the Ghost grew older, clearly older.

'Are spirits' lives so short?' asked Scrooge.

'My life in this world is very brief,' replied the Ghost. 'It ends tonight.'

'Tonight!' cried Scrooge.

'At the stroke of midnight. Hark! The time draws near.'

The chimes were ringing three-quarters past eleven at that moment. And as they rang, Scrooge noticed something strange, something that might have been a foot or might have been a claw, protruding from

the Spirit's robe. He asked the Spirit what
it was.

'Behold!' cried the Ghost.

Parting the folds of its robe, it revealed
two children, wretched, ragged, miserable
children, a boy and a girl, all skin and
bone, who knelt fearfully at its feet clinging
to its garment.

Scrooge started back, appalled. Having
them shown to him in this way, he tried to

say that they were fine children, but the words choked themselves rather than come out in a lie.

'Spirit, are these children yours?'

'They are Man's,' said the Spirit, placing a hand on either head. 'This boy is Ignorance. This girl is Want. Beware of them both, but most of all, beware this boy.'

'But have they no refuge?' cried Scrooge. 'Is there nowhere they can hide?'

'Are there no prisons?' said the Spirit, turning on him for the last time with his own words. 'Are there no workhouses?'

The bell struck twelve.

Scrooge looked about him for the Ghost, and saw it not. As the last stroke ceased to vibrate, he recalled the prediction of old Jacob Marley, and, lifting up his eyes, beheld a solemn Phantom, draped and hooded, coming like a mist along the ground towards him.

What did Bob Cratchit and his family, and Fred and his friends think about Scrooge?

4
The Last of the Spirits

The Phantom slowly, gravely, silently approached. When it came near him, Scrooge bent down upon his knee; for this Spirit seemed to scatter gloom and mystery in the very air through which it moved.

It was shrouded in a deep black garment which concealed its head, its face, its form, and left nothing of it visible save one outstretched hand. But for this it would have been difficult to separate the figure from the darkness by which it was surrounded.

When at last it stood beside him, the Phantom seemed to Scrooge tall and stately, and its mysterious presence filled him with a solemn dread.

'Am I in the presence of the Ghost of Christmas Yet to Come?' he asked.

The Spirit answered not, but pointed onward with its hand.

'You are about to show me shadows of things that have not yet happened, but will happen in the time before us,' Scrooge pursued.

Again the Spirit gave no reply, but the upper portion of its garment moved as if in a small nod of agreement.

Although well used to ghostly company by this time, Scrooge feared the silent shape so much that his legs trembled beneath him, and he found that he could hardly stand when he prepared to follow it. The Spirit paused a moment, giving him time to recover.

But Scrooge was all the worse for this. It thrilled him with a vague, uncertain horror to know that, behind the dusky shroud, ghostly eyes were fixed intently upon him, while his own eyes could see nothing but that spectral hand and one great heap of black.

'Ghost of the Future!' he exclaimed. 'I fear you more than any Spectre I have seen. But as I know your purpose is to do me good, I bear your company with a thankful heart. Now will you not speak to me?'

The Ghost gave no reply. The hand was pointed straight before them.

'Well then,' sighed Scrooge, 'lead on. The night is waning fast and I know that time is precious to me. Lead on, Spirit!'

The Phantom moved away as it had come towards him. Scrooge followed in the shadow of its robe, which seemed to bear him up and carry him along.

They had not gone far before the city sprang up about them. And then they were in the heart of it, among the merchants, who hurried up and down and chinked the money in their pockets, and conversed in small groups, and looked at their watches, as Scrooge had so often seen them do.

The Spirit stopped beside one little knot of business men. Scrooge knew the men. Observing that the hand pointed at them, he advanced to listen to their talk.

'When did he die?' inquired one man of another.

'Last night, I believe,' returned a great

fat man with a monstrous chin.

'I thought he'd never die, that one,' said a third, taking a vast quantity of snuff from a very large snuff box. 'What was the matter with him?'

The man with the large chin yawned. 'I don't know much about it. Only that he's dead.'

'What's to become of his money?' asked a red-faced man with an unflattering growth on the end of his nose.

'I haven't heard,' said the one with the chin. 'He hasn't left it to me, I know that much.'

This was received with a general laugh.

'It's likely to be a very cheap funeral,' the same man went on, 'for upon my life I don't know anybody who would go to it. Suppose we make up a party and volunteer?'

'I don't mind going if lunch is provided,' observed the gentleman with the bulbous nose. 'I must be fed.'

Another laugh, and then the party strolled away and mixed with other groups.

Scrooge looked towards the Spirit for an explanation. The Phantom gave none, but glided on, into another busy street, where it pointed at two gentlemen meeting there. These two also were men of business known to Scrooge. Both were very wealthy, and of great importance.

'Well!' said one. 'The old boy has met his end at last, eh?'

'So I'm told,' returned the second. 'Cold, isn't it?'

'Seasonable for Christmas time. You are not a skater, I suppose?'

'No, no. Other things to think of. Good morning to you!'

Not another word. Scrooge was surprised that the Spirit should attach importance to such trivial conversations, but certain that he was made to hear them for his own good, he resolved to remember everything he heard, as well as everything he saw.

The Spirit stood beside him, quiet and dark, its hand still stretched out before it. Scrooge fancied that the unseen eyes were gazing at him keenly. He shuddered, and felt very cold.

They left the busy scene and went into another part of town, a part that Scrooge had never visited before, although he recognized it from its bad reputation. The streets were narrow and foul, the shops and houses wretched, the people in rags, drunken, careless and ugly. Alleys and archways spewed forth unpleasant smells and dirt, and the whole quarter reeked of crime and filth and misery.

At the heart of this bleak area, there stood a low-roofed shop, where iron, old rags, bottles, bones and greasy offal were bought and sold. It was a kind of place that Scrooge would never have entered of his own accord, but the Spirit guided him inside. There, upon the floor, were piled heaps of rough iron of all kinds: rusty keys, nails, chains, hinges, scales, weights, and more. Secrets that few would care to scrutinize were hidden in mountains of stinking rags and gloomy hills of bones. Sitting among these wares, by a charcoal stove made of old bricks, was a grey-haired old rascal, calmly smoking a pipe.

Scrooge and the Phantom came into the presence of this man, just as a woman with a heavy bundle slunk into the shop. She herself had scarcely entered when another woman, similarly laden, came in too; and she was closely followed by a man in faded black, who was no less startled by the sight of them than they had been on seeing one another. After a short period of blank astonishment, in which the old man with the pipe joined them, they all three burst into a laugh.

'Well look here, old Joe,' cried the woman who had entered first. 'What a chance! The charwoman, the laundress, and the undertaker, all three met here without meaning it!'

'You couldn't have met in a better place,' said old Joe, removing the pipe from his mouth. 'Come into the parlour now.'

The parlour was a space behind a screen of rags and there the proprietor invited his visitors to show him what they'd brought. The woman who had first arrived threw her bundle on the floor and sat down on a stool, crossing her elbows on her knees and casting a bold glance at the other two, not least the second woman.

'What of it, Mrs Dilber?' she said. 'Every person has a right to take care of themselves. *He* always did!'

'That's true indeed!' said the laundress. 'No man more so.'

'Why then, don't stand there staring as if you was afraid, woman! Who's the wiser? And who's the worse for the loss of a few things like these? Not a dead man, that's certain!'

'No indeed,' said Mrs Dilber, laughing.

'If he wanted to keep 'em after he was dead, the wicked old devil,' the woman went on, 'why wasn't he natural in his lifetime? If he had been, he'd have had somebody to look after him when he was struck with Death, instead of lying gasping out his last there, alone by himself.'

'A truer word was never spoke,' said Mrs Dilber. 'It's a judgment on him.'

'I wish it was a little heavier judgment,' replied the charwoman. 'If there'd been more, I would have laid my hands on it, you may depend upon it. Now who shall go first?'

The man in faded black, the undertaker, produced his plunder. It was not much. A pencil case, a pair of sleeve buttons, a brooch, a few other trifles, nothing of great value. They were looked over by old Joe, who chalked the fee he was prepared to pay upon the wall.

'I wouldn't give another sixpence,' he said. 'Not if I was to be boiled for not doing it. Next.'

Mrs Dilber was next. Sheets and towels,

a little clothing, two old-fashioned silver teaspoons, a pair of sugar tongs, and some pairs of boots. Her account was chalked upon the wall in the same way.

'I always give too much to the ladies,' Joe said. 'It's a weakness of mine. But if you asked me for another penny, and made an argument of it, I'd be bound to change my mind and knock off half a crown.'

'Now undo my bundle,' commanded the first woman.

Old Joe went down on his knees and, having unfastened a great many knots, dragged out a large roll of dark material.

'What's this? Bed curtains? You don't mean to say you took 'em down, rings and all, with him lying there?'

'I do,' said the charwoman, leaning forward on her crossed arms. 'Why not?'

'You were born to make your fortune,' said Joe, 'and you'll certainly do it.'

'I shan't hold back when I can get something by reaching for it,' the woman answered coolly. 'Not for the sake of such a man as he was. Now, Joe, what do you say to those blankets?'

'*His* blankets?' asked Joe.

'Whose else's do you think?' replied the

char. 'He ain't likely to feel the cold
without 'em, I dare say.'

Old Joe inspected the blankets. 'I hope
he didn't die of anything catching, that's all.'

'Don't you be afraid of that,' the woman
said. 'I ain't so fond of his company as I'd
loiter about him if he did.'

'And his nightshirt too!' exclaimed Joe
in amazement.

'Ah! You may look through that shirt till
your eyes ache, but you won't find a hole
in it, nor a threadbare place. It's the best
he had, and a fine one too. They'd have
wasted it, if it hadn't been for me.'

'What do you call wasting it?' asked old
Joe.

'Putting it on him to be buried in,' the woman replied with a laugh. 'Somebody was fool enough to do it, but I took it off again and put another on him.'

Scrooge listened to this dialogue in horror. As these four sat grouped about their spoils in the scanty light of the old man's lamp, he viewed them with a disgust which could hardly have been greater had they been haggling over the corpse itself.

'Well, this is the end of it,' said the charwoman when old Joe produced a bag of money and counted out each payment on the floor. 'He frightened everyone away when he was alive, to profit us when he was dead! Ha, ha, ha!'

'Spirit!' said Scrooge, shuddering from head to foot. 'I see your meaning. The case of this unhappy man might be my own. My life goes that way now, but... Oh! Merciful Heaven, what is *this*?'

He recoiled in terror, for the scene had changed, and now he almost touched a bed – a bare, uncurtained bed – on which, beneath a ragged sheet, something lay covered up. The room was very dark, too dark to make much out with any certainty, but then, a pale light rose in the air and

fell upon the bed; and on it, robbed,
unwatched, unmourned, uncared for, was
the body of a man.

The Phantom's steady hand was
pointed at the head. The bed cover was so
carelessly placed that the flick of a finger
would have removed it. Scrooge thought of
this, but he had no more power to
withdraw the veil than to dismiss the
Spectre at his side.

'Spirit!' he said. 'This is a fearful place.
In leaving it, I shall not leave its lesson,
trust me. Let us go!'

Still the Ghost pointed with a steady
finger to the head.

'I understand you,' said Scrooge, 'and I
would do it if I could. But I have not the

power to remove it. I have not the power.'

Again, the Spirit's unseen eyes seemed fixed upon him from within the dusky shroud.

'Spirit,' said Scrooge, 'if there is any person in town who feels emotion at this man's death, I beseech you, show that person to me!'

At this, the Phantom spread its dark robe before him for a moment, like a wing; and, withdrawing it, revealed a room by daylight, where a mother and her children were.

The mother was expecting someone. She walked up and down the room, started at every sound, looked out of the window, glanced at the clock. At length, the long-expected knock was heard. She hurried to the door and met her husband: a man whose face was careworn and depressed, though he was young.

He sat down to the dinner that had been waiting for him by the fire, and when his wife asked him faintly for his news he seemed uncertain how to answer.

'Well?' she said. 'Is it good or bad?'

'Not good,' he answered.

'We are quite ruined?'

'Perhaps not. There is hope yet, Caroline.'

'If he relents, there is,' his wife replied. 'If he changes his mind, there is.' But then she stared at him, amazed. 'Can such a miracle have happened?'

'He is past relenting,' said her husband. 'He is dead.'

'Dead? But our debt. To whom will it be transferred?'

'I don't know, but before that time we'll be ready with the money. And even if we were not, it would be bad fortune indeed if the one who takes his place were such a hard man. I think we may sleep with light hearts tonight, Caroline!'

The children clustered round. They understood little of what had passed between their parents, but their faces were brighter, their hearts lighter, and it was a happier house for this man's death.

'Spirit,' said Scrooge, 'let me see some tenderness connected with death, or that dark room which we just left will be for ever with me.'

The Ghost then conducted him through several familiar streets, and as they went Scrooge looked here and there for his future self. Nowhere was he to be seen.

At last they entered Bob Cratchit's house, the same dwelling they had visited before but so changed that Scrooge could only stare. The children sat with their mother near the fire, as still as statues. Mrs Cratchit and her daughters were engaged in sewing, while Master Peter read a book. And all of them so quiet, so very quiet.

Mrs Cratchit laid her work upon the table and put her hand up to her face.

'The candle-light hurts my eyes,' she said. 'I mustn't show red eyes to your father when he comes home. It must be near his time.'

'Past it rather,' Peter answered. 'But I think he's walked a little slower than he used to, these last few evenings.'

They fell quiet again. At last, the mother said, in a steady, cheerful voice that only faltered once: 'I have known him walk very fast indeed with... with Tiny Tim upon his shoulder.'

'So have I,' said Peter. 'Often.'

'So have I,' exclaimed another. And so had all.

'But he was very light to carry,' she continued, 'and his father loved him so, that it was no trouble at all.'

'There's father now,' said Peter.

Mrs Cratchit hurried out to meet him, and brought him in to sit beside the fire. The two young Cratchits got up on their father's knees and laid, each child, a cheek against his face, as if to say, 'Don't mind, father. Don't grieve.'

Bob was very cheerful with them, and spoke pleasantly to all the family. He looked at the sewing work and praised his wife and daughters. But then, silence returned.

'You've been to the grave, haven't you, Robert?' his wife said.

'Yes, my dear,' confessed Bob. 'And I wish you had been there with me. It would have done you good to see how green a place it is. But you'll see it often. I promised him we would walk there every Sunday. Oh, my child! My little, little child!'

He broke down all at once. He couldn't help it. He left the room and went upstairs. Silence came again, but very soon Bob returned, composed and cheerful once more.

The family drew about the fire and talked, the girls and mother working still. Bob told them of the kindness of Mr Scrooge's nephew, who, meeting him in the street earlier and seeing that he was a little down, inquired what had happened to him.

'Well,' said Bob, 'I told him that Tiny Tim had died, and the young gentleman said that he was heartily sorry, and he gave me his card, and said "That's where I live. If I can be of service to you in any way, pray come to me." '

'He sounds like a good soul,' said Mrs Cratchit.

'You would be sure of it, my dear,' returned Bob, 'if you saw and spoke to him. He was so concerned that it seemed as if he had known our Tim, and felt the loss with us.'

Once again, the family drew together in the firelight, and silence fell among them. The scene began to fade.

'Spectre,' said Scrooge, 'something tells me that our parting is at hand. Before the moment comes, pray tell me what man it was whom we saw lying dead.'

The Ghost of Christmas Yet to Come conveyed him away from that place to another. They stood before the iron gate of a churchyard. Here, then, the wretched man whose name he would now learn, lay beneath the ground. Walled in by tall dark houses, overrun by grass and weeds, the crop of death, not life. A worthy place indeed!

The Spirit stood among the graves, and pointed down to one in particular. Scrooge advanced towards it, trembling; but hesitated.

'Before I draw near that stone,' he said, 'answer me one question. Are these the shadows of things that Will be, or merely the shadows of what May be?'

Still the Ghost pointed downward to the grave by which it stood.

Scrooge crept forward, trembling as he went; and, following the finger, read the name upon the stone of the neglected grave: EBENEZER SCROOGE.

With a moan, he fell to his knees before the Phantom. 'Am I the man who lay upon the bed?' he said.

The finger pointed from the grave to him, and back again.

'No, Spirit! Oh no, no!'

Scrooge clutched tight at the ghostly robe.

'Spirit, hear me! I am not the man I was. I will not be the man I've been till now. Why show me this if I am past all hope?'

For the first time the Spirit's hand appeared unsteady.

'Good Spirit,' Scrooge pursued from his knees, tugging at the Phantom's dark robe, 'I believe that you pity me. Assure me that I yet may change these shadows you have shown me!'

The kind hand trembled.

'I will honour Christmas with all my heart,' Scrooge said, 'and try to keep it all year round. I will live in the Past, the Present, and the Future. The Spirits of all three shall live within me. I will not forget the lessons that they teach. Oh, tell me I may wipe away the writing on this stone!'

In his misery he caught the spectral hand and held it with all his might. The Spirit, stronger still, shook him off. But then, holding up his hands in a last prayer to have his fate reversed, Scrooge saw a change in the Phantom's hood and robe. It withered, collapsed, and dwindled down – into a bedpost.

Why did Scrooge promise to honour Christmas after he was visited by the Ghost of Christmas Yet to Come?

5
The End of It

Yes, the bedpost was his own! The bed was his own, the room was his own. Best and happiest of all, the time before him was his own, to make amends in!

'I will live in the Past, the Present, and the Future!' Scrooge repeated as he scrambled out of bed. 'The Spirits of all Three shall live within me. O Jacob Marley! Heaven and Christmas time be praised for this! I say it on my knees, Jacob. On my knees!'

He had been sobbing violently before the last Spirit, and his face was wet with tears. But now he was so flustered, and so glowing with good intentions, and his voice was so broken with emotion, that he was for a minute all a'twitter.

'I don't know what to do!' he said, laughing and crying in the same breath. 'I am as light as a feather, I am as happy as an angel, I am as merry as a schoolboy! A Merry Christmas to everyone! A Happy New Year to all the world! Hullo there! Whoop! Hullo!'

He frisked about the room, touching his possessions, his garments, his ornaments, marvelling at all as he had never marvelled at them before.

'There's the door by which the Spirit of Jacob Marley entered! There's the corner where the Ghost of Christmas Present sat! There's the window where I saw the wandering Spirits! It's all right, it's all true, it all happened. Ha, ha, ha!'

For a man who had been out of practice for so many years, it was a splendid laugh, a most illustrious laugh, the father of a long, long line of utterly brilliant laughs!

'I don't know what day of the month it is,' said Scrooge, quite out of breath with all this scurrying and laughing. 'I don't know how long I've been among the Spirits. I don't know anything. I'm quite a baby. Well I don't care. I'd rather be a baby. Hullo! Whoop! Hullo-ho-ho!'

Running to the window, he opened it and put out his head. No fog, no mist. Cold, clear, bright, cheery. Golden sunlight, heavenly sky, sweet fresh air, merry bells. Oh, glorious, glorious!

'You boy!' Scrooge called to a boy passing below. 'What day is it?'

'Eh?' said the boy, looking up in wonder.

'What's today, my fine fellow?'

'Today? Why, it's Christmas Day!'

'Christmas Day!' said Scrooge. 'It's Christmas Day. I haven't missed it. The Spirits have done it all in one night! Well, well!' He leaned out once more. 'Do you know the poulterer's in the high street, the one on the corner?'

'Course I do,' replied the lad.

'An intelligent boy!' said Scrooge. 'A remarkable boy! Do you know if they've sold the prize turkey hanging up there? Not the little prize turkey, the big one.'

'The one as big as me?' answered the boy.

'What a delightful boy!' said Scrooge. 'Pleasure to talk to him. Yes, my lad, that's the one.'

'It's still there,' said the boy.

'Good, good, good,' said Scrooge. 'I'd like you to go and buy it for me.'

'Buy it for you?'

'Go and buy it, and tell 'em to bring it here, that I may give them directions where to take it. Come back with the man and I'll give you a shilling. Come back with him in less than five minutes and I'll give you half a crown!'

The boy was off like a shot.

Scrooge rubbed his hands with glee. 'I'll send it to Bob Cratchit,' he said to himself. 'He won't know who it came from. He'll have no idea!'

The hand in which he wrote Bob's address was not a steady one, but write it he did, somehow, and when it was done he went downstairs to open the street door, ready for the coming turkey. As he stood there waiting, the knocker caught his eye.

'What a wonderful knocker!' he cried, patting it lightly. 'A veritable *king* among knockers! Ah! Here's the turkey. Hullo! Whoop! How are you! Merry Christmas!'

And it *was* a turkey! So great, so fat, so enormous, that it never could have stood upon legs. They would have snapped off in a minute.

'Why, it's impossible to carry that fellow to Camden Town,' said Scrooge to the man. 'You must have a cab!'

The chuckle with which he said this, and the chuckle with which he paid for the turkey and the cab, and the chuckle with which he settled up with the boy, were only exceeded when he sat down breathless afterwards and chuckled till he cried.

He dressed himself all in his best and went out into the streets. By this time, people were pouring forth and Scrooge regarded every one with a delighted smile. He had not gone far when he beheld, coming towards him, one of the two gentlemen who had entered his counting-house the day before; the one who had said 'Scrooge and Marley's, I believe?'

'My dear sir,' said Scrooge, quickening his pace and taking the gentleman by both hands, 'how do you do? A merry Christmas to you, sir!'

'Mr Scrooge?'

'It is I,' said Scrooge. 'Allow me to beg your pardon for my behaviour yesterday. I would like to make amends.'

And here Scrooge whispered in his ear.

'Lord bless me!' cried the gentleman,

astonished. 'My dear Mr Scrooge, so
much? Are you serious?'

'I am, sir,' returned Scrooge. 'Not a
penny less. Come and see me and you shall
have it without delay.'

They went their separate ways. Scrooge
walked about the streets and watched the
people hurrying to and fro. He patted
children on the head, and looked into
kitchens and up at Christmas windows, and
found that everything gave him pleasure.
Everything!

In the afternoon he turned towards his
nephew's house. He passed the door a
dozen times before he found the courage
to knock.

'Why, bless my soul!' cried the young
man when he saw him on the step. 'Uncle
Scrooge!'

'Fred!' said Scrooge. 'I have come to dinner. Will you let me in?'

'Let you in?' said Fred. 'Why, I should say so!'

And he shook Scrooge's hand so hard it was a mercy he didn't shake it off. He took his uncle inside, and how his young wife did start! But Scrooge was made welcome and felt at home in five minutes. Nothing could be heartier. Scrooge had never had such a Christmas Day, and was the life and soul of the party.

But he was early at the office next morning. He made a point of it, to catch Bob Cratchit coming late. And so he did.

The clock struck nine. No Bob. A quarter past. No Bob. Scrooge sat with his door wide open so that he might see him come in. He arrived a full eighteen and a half minutes late. His hat was off before he opened the door, and he was on his stool in a jiffy, driving away with his pen to make up for the time lost.

'Hullo!' growled Scrooge in his usual voice. 'What do you mean by coming here at this time of day?'

'I'm very sorry, sir,' said Bob.

'I should think you are!' said Scrooge.

'Step this way, sir, if you please!'

'It's only once a year, sir,' pleaded Bob, entering Scrooge's office. 'It shall not be repeated. I was making rather merry yesterday. You see, someone delivered a turkey to us, and –'

'I'll tell you what, my friend,' Scrooge interrupted. 'I'm not going to stand this sort of thing any longer. And therefore,' he continued, leaping from his stool and digging Bob hard in the ribs, 'and therefore I am going to…raise your salary!'

'What?' said Bob, staggering.

'Merry Christmas, Bob!' cried Scrooge with a hearty change of voice. He clapped his clerk on the back. 'A merrier Christmas, my good fellow, than I've given you for

many a year! I'll raise your salary, and assist your struggling family, and we will discuss your affairs this very afternoon over a Christmas bowl of punch. But for now, Bob Cratchit, make up the fires and buy another coal scuttle before you even dot another "i"!'

Scrooge was better than his word. He did it all, and infinitely more. And to Tiny Tim, who did not die, he was a second father. He became as good a friend, as good a master, and as good a man as could be found anywhere. Some people laughed to see the change in him, but he let them laugh and minded not at all, and even joined them in their laughter.

He had no further dealings with Spirits, but it was always said of Ebenezer Scrooge from that day forth that he knew how to keep Christmas well. May that be truly said of all of us. And as Tiny Tim observed, God bless Us, Every One!

What issues does Dickens raise in this story?